MW00986106

The Strict Teachers

Madison is spanked by two experienced teachers
By Paula Mann
Spanking Bedside Stories Series

Published by Mann Publishing

Copyright © 2021 Paula Mann

Contents

The Strict Teachers

Miss Smith Punished Madison for Failing her Exam

This is the third story about Madison Hunter. I suggest that you read "The Strict Landlady" and "The Strict Mother-in-law" first, but you don't need to if that's not your thing. This story works on its own.

Paula

x

Mike and I got married again in October, exactly four years after our first marriage and just one year after our divorce, and we moved into a lovely flat with an ornate balcony that was purchased for us as a wedding present. We were always friends and we had fallen in love again after Mike's parents, Mr and Mrs Hunter, had started to spank us regularly when we both lived with them. The simple ritual happened on a Saturday night when Mr Hunter was home from working in London all week. The two dining chairs would be placed in the lounge facing each other. When Mr and Mrs Hunter were seated Mike and I would strip naked and stand waiting to be told what to do. I would usually be over Mrs Hunter's lap to start and Mike over his Father's. After ten minutes of spanking, we would have to stand in the corner showing off our little red bottoms, my long blond hair flowing down my back and then swap spankers for another ten minutes over the other person's knee. We would both be in tears after the spanking but Mr and Mrs Hunter would rush upstairs to their bedroom, leaving Mike and I to enjoy the aftermath of the spanking and then make glorious love.

This worked so well that it continued when we moved into the new flat. Mr and Mrs Hunter bought us a new dining table and four chairs so that there were always good strong dining chairs to sit on when they spanked us. Although we are in our mid-twenties, Mike and I are both short at five foot two inches, and slim with small bottoms so it was easy for Mr and Mrs Hunter to have us over their knee.

Alas, this didn't last long and when Mr Hunter took a senior position in a bank in Cape Town, South Africa, Mrs Hunter sold the house and went with him, leaving Mike and I on our own. We tried spanking each other but that just didn't work at all and by Christmas, we were arguing again.

In the meantime, I had been studying a basic course in Human Resources. The course started very well, but with the marriage and moving into a new flat on top of my typing job in an office, I failed one of the exams. Miss Smith, responsible for adult education in Bournemouth, had taken an interest in me and I would see her every second week to tell her how I was getting on. When I visited her in her office at the town hall after I had failed that exam, she didn't look at all pleased with me.

"That should have been an easy exam for you Madison. What happened?" she said.

"I am so sorry Miss Smith," I said. "I got married and we moved into a new flat. It took all my time."

"Okay, Madison." Miss Smith said. "That is the excuse, but what is the real reason you failed?"

I started to cry and Miss Smith came around her desk and put a hand on my shoulder. "Well?" she said.

I thought for a while and then said, "Yes, you are right. I knew I would pass so I think I didn't study hard enough." I said. "I was horrified that I didn't even understand the questions, let alone be able to answer them."

"That's better," Miss Smith said. "You know I don't usually take this much interest in the girls who come here to study, don't you?"

"Yes, I know," I said.

"And I have far too many other things to think

about, other than a lazy girl who does not want to pass exams," she said. "I think you had better get going now. No need to make more appointments to see me regularly."

Miss Smith was standing next to me and I took her hand. "No please Miss Smith. I made a mistake, but that will be the last one, I promise."

Miss Smith sat on her desk next to me. "How can I be sure I am not wasting my time, Madison Hunter?" she said.

I was still crying but from my seated position I looked straight up into her face. My makeup must have been streaming down my face and I probably looked like a wreck. "I don't know Miss Smith," I said. "I will do whatever you tell me to do."

Miss Smith was thoughtful for a while. "Okay," she said. "You will be punished for not passing that Exam and then we will set you some tough targets for the month. You will study hard and if you don't hit the target there will be more punishment. Do you agree?"

"Yes of course," I said. "But what sort of punishment would that be?" I had a feeling I knew what sort of punishment it would be because Miss Smith had patted my bottom when I left the first time I had met her, but I just wanted it confirmed.

"Well, you were naughty when you didn't study hard for that exam weren't you?" She asked.

"Yes, I was," I said.

"And what happens to naughty girls?" Miss Smith asked

"Well," I said. "If they are naughty little girls they usually get spanked,"

"Stand up Madison." Miss Smith said in a commanding voice. "Kick off your heels and stand straight." I was not sure what was happening but I did as I was told and stood there in my short white dress and bare feet and standing close Miss Smith towered over me. "How tall are you Madison?"

"I am not sure." I lied.

"That lie has just earned you extra punishment, so I will ask again." Miss Smith said.

"I am five foot two inches, Miss Smith," I said.

"And at five foot two inches, would you say that you are a little girl?" she asked.

I was feeling very little right now and so I just nodded.

"Right. We have agreed that not studying hard for that exam was naughty. And we have also agreed, and it is plain to see, that you are a little girl. So by definition what sort of punishment are you going to get?" Miss Smith was smiling now, like a cat that had just cornered a mouse.

"I think I am probably going to get spanked, Miss Smith," I said.

"Clever girl." Miss Smith said. "Today I am going to spank you quite hard over my desk for not passing that easy exam. Then we are going to set you some tough targets and we will meet here every second Tuesday evening after you finish work, and you will get another spanking if you have not completed the work to my satisfaction. You will be able to sit the exam in five months and I can assure you will get over eighty per cent. Any questions?"

"No, Miss Smith," I said. "And thank you for taking the time to correct my behaviour. But…"

"But what?" she asked.

"I am having difficulty studying at home. My husband doesn't like it, and I am trying to better myself. He says that I should just have a few babies to keep me busy at home. I will have to find somewhere else to study, I think, but I know I deserve to be spanked now."

"You may not be saying that when I have finished with you today." Miss Smith said. "I am angry with you and I expect it will show on your bottom when I have finished. Now get across the desk diagonally with the corner of the desk between your legs. That will hold you in place while I punish you"

"Yes Miss Smith," I said. "Like this?" I was bending

over Miss Smith's desk stretching across diagonally. I had never been in this position before and it felt very strange.

"No Madison." Miss Smith said. "Get closer to the desk so that the corner of the desk is between your legs." I adjusted my position. "Closer," she said.

I was now as close to the desk as I could get and the corner of the desk was between my legs and sticking out the other side. I had to spread my legs to get as close as she wanted, but I was short so I had to get on my tiptoes to get into position. Once I stood on my feet again my pussy was right against the desk. "Oh," I said.

"That's it, my girl," she said. "How does that feel?"

"A little strange Miss Smith," I said, but I didn't want to tell her that it made me feel a little horny as well.

Miss Smith walked around her desk and picked up a wicked looking ruler. It was about sixty centimetres in length and about five centimetres in width. It was made of wood and had seen a lot of service in its day I would think.

"Do you know what this is Madison?" she asked.

"No Miss Smith," I said.

"This, my girl, is the old school ruler I used to use on the old blackboards to draw straight lines with chalk, and on bottoms to leave straight welts for the children to take home with them." She said, "It was such fun."

"Oh," I said and I was not sure this was going to be any fun at all.

She walked back around her desk and said. "Lift up your skirt Madison and I will let you keep your knickers on this time, but be warned, they are coming down if there is a next time I have to punish you."

"Yes, Miss Smith," I said. "And thank you,"

The nasty-looking ruler descended on my bottom six times, but Miss Smith was plainly not putting her best effort into the strokes. I expect she wasn't aware that I am used to being spanked. "Miss Smith," I said.

"Yes, Madison,"

"I have been spanked and caned often, I am sure you can give me six more hard strokes if you think I deserve it."

Miss Smith laughed, as she smoothed down the white cotton material of my knickers. "So who has spanked you Madison?"

"Quite a few people really, Mrs Johnson, she was my landlady. Mrs Hunter, my ex-mother-in-law. Her husband as well sometimes." I said.

"Not your husband then?" she asked.

"Good Lord no," I said. "Well, we did try once but he prefers to be spanked."

"I can see why Mrs Trent recommended you to me now," Miss Smith said, but she didn't elaborate. "Well six more then, and this time I won't be soft on you."

"Thank you, Miss Smith," I said as the first of the six landed on my knickers. "Phew, that ruler can sting," I said, but Miss Smith didn't answer, just delivered the last five.

I was crying when Miss Smith finished, and she slipped the box of tissues across the desk towards me. "You took those very well Madison." Miss Smith said. "Do you mind if I have a look?"

I sniffed as I reached behind me and eased down my knickers over my sore bottom.

"You are a brave girl Madison," Miss Smith said as she patted my bottom. "This bottom will sting for a while I think, but I have a feeling that this will not be the last time I spank it. I see your pussy has left a big damp patch on your knickers and your skirt. That will be hard to hide on your way home, maybe we should spank you with your knickers off and your dress out the way next time."

"Yes, Thank you, Miss Smith," I said. "I think it was having my pussy over the corner of the desk, every stroke of the ruler pushed me forwards."

"Yes, I understand," Miss Smith said. "I will drive you home this time so you are not embarrassed by the stain on your dress."

"Thank you, Miss Smith," I said.

Trouble with the Young Hunters

When Miss Smith dropped me off she told me that she lived just around the corner with her partner, so maybe I should go there in the evening to study if I find it difficult at home.

"Oh I couldn't do that Miss Smith," I said. "That would be an imposition, anyway I am sure your partner wouldn't like that, what would he say?"

"What would she say, you mean," she said.

"Oh, of course, sorry," I said, but I was uncertain what to say.

Miss Smith reached across and held my hand. "No matter," she said. "And I am sure she wouldn't mind either." We both smiled at each other as I got out of the car. Then I waved and walked up the stairs to the block of flats.

I was smiling when I got home but it wasn't really home now. Mike was not good at tidying his things so the house was a mess, and he had started staying out late most evenings, drinking in the pub on his way home from work. He had got quite a good job now as a salesman earning good money, but there was very little at the end of the month for groceries and the like. I complained that I seemed to be buying all the necessary stuff with my money and he was just spending his on drink. We didn't argue for long and he would just go to the spare bedroom and slam the door.

In the past when my in-laws were just around the corner we could go there and get spanked. That always excited both of us and the lovemaking afterwards was very nice. Now they are in Cape Town and we would not see them for another year or more. My orgasms with Mike were not as good as I had with Mrs Johnson or as long-lasting as with Mrs Hunter, but we were making love just like men and women should do, and that meant something, I guess.

The last time we were married we dragged it out for three years before we got divorced but this time I was determined that we wouldn't waste all that time with endless arguments about nothing.

I made myself some supper and watched TV mindlessly. I couldn't tell you what was on because I wasn't really paying attention. Mike came home at about nine and he had obviously been drinking but he wasn't really drunk.

"I got a big contract today," he said. "I may have to go to Glasgow to set it all up, we will see."

"Okay, Mike, well done," I said.

"I don't think you understand, you will be coming with me to Glasgow, we can sell this flat and rent a place up there," he said. "Then you can concentrate on having some babies."

I was horrified. "I will certainly not be coming to Glasgow with you, in fact, I would be very happy if you go on your own and never come back." It was my turn to go to the bedroom and slam the door, then I sat on the bed and cried.

I was awake late that night trying to work things out. Mike and I were great together as friends, but not as a married couple. The trouble was that we both liked being submissive. I was shy and inexperienced when I met Mike in the restaurant where we both worked nearly five years ago. I thought I had really found the love of my life, so we were married at the end of the summer season, and then it all started to go wrong.

It was only when I was spanked by Mrs Johnson in my digs, that I really discovered the meaning of the word orgasm. It was the same with Mrs Hunter, and I loved giving her pleasure as well. Then there was Miss Smith today. She had used that ruler on my bottom and I had soaked my knickers. She said she has a female partner, so she is a lesbian. I sat up in bed, "Am I a lesbian?"

I know what you are thinking, "Duh," Of course I should have known, but I was brought up in a very straight homophobic household, it was just a way of life. People just didn't do that sort of thing.

I remember enjoying looking at the other girls in the school showers, but doesn't everybody? Then when a nice girl walks past me in the street wearing tight pants I look, of course. But to be perfectly honest, I don't look at boys in the same way. I do what I have to do as a wife with Mike's penis, but please don't ask me if I like it. Mrs Hunter's pussy, however, especially after she trimmed her hair. Now that, I could play with all night, if I got the chance, and I often did.

So I am a lesbian then. I love the idea of being spanked by a woman. Miss Smith would do very nicely. Then maybe pleasuring her if she wants me to. I would like that.

I fell asleep with that pleasant thought.

I was sitting at the breakfast table when Mike came into the kitchen and he looked wrecked. He was the first to talk as he switched on the kettle. "Sorry about last night," he said. "This opportunity in Glasgow has been on the skyline for a few weeks but I knew you wouldn't like it so I didn't mention it until I was sure. It will be good for both of us to go somewhere new and then, if we sell the house, we would both have some cash in the bank."

I was annoyed of course, but I was trying to keep calm. "I will not be going to Glasgow with you Mike, and I think we should separate as soon as we can. This isn't working and all we have done is to spoil a good friendship by getting married just like last time. Let's just call it quits."

"Okay," he said rather too quickly, "but we have to sell the flat. I need the money."

"What on earth do you need money for, you have a good salary," I said.

"I have got into a little debt," he said. "Poker."

"Oh, Mike, you bloody fool," I said. "How much?"

Mike was not so happy now. "Ten thousand pounds, just a little over," he said.

I wasn't going to cry, not this time. One of us had to be strong, so I sent Mike off to work with the promise that he will come straight home this evening. Then I called my boss and told her that I am sick and I will not be at work today. "I have the flu," I sniffed.

The first thing I did was to get out the paperwork for the flat. It was a wedding present from Mr and Mrs Hunter, but I knew Mr Hunter would have sorted the details. I took the documents out of the cashbox where I kept this sort of thing and read it through.

The flat was purchased for four hundred and twenty thousand pounds and there was no mortgage, so there was plenty of capital in the flat, but I didn't want to sell it. I was sure that the flat would have been bought in Mike's name as it was his father who financed it, but, when I got to the ownership page it was in my name, not in Mike's or both our names. Just mine.

To say I was shocked would be an understatement. Mr Hunter and I had shared a secret last year, and if it had come out there would have been serious problems in the Hunter household, so I kept my mouth shut. I think this was Mr Hunter's way of saying thank you. Mr Hunter had given me his office address and phone number in Cape town just in case there were any problems so I thought this would be the time to call him. It was a difficult call.

After the usual preliminaries, I got straight to the point. "Mr Hunter. I have been going through the paperwork and I see the flat you gave us as a wedding present is actually in my name, why is that?"

"Ah, yes," he said. "If you have discovered that, it probably means that you are having money problems over there."

I told Mr Hunter everything including the breakdown in the marriage and the gambling debt.

Then Mr Hunter said, "Are you asking for my advice, Madison?"

"I guess so," I said.

"If I was you I would kick Mike out of your flat and let him go to Glasgow. Tell him to call me and I will give him ten thousand pounds to bail him out again, but this will be the last time. It is not the first time, I don't expect you knew that." Mr Hunter said.

"No, I didn't," I said.

"That's why the flat is in your name." Mr Hunter said. "You keep it my darling. I owe you a lot, I think you know that. So now we are even." He was laughing when he said that, and I felt relieved.

After that call, I worked out what to say to Mike. I didn't want to be married to a gambler and if his father was going to pay his debts, well that's okay.

When Mike came home that evening at six he had already had a drink so he must have left work early. "Well," he said, "How much is the flat worth?"

"We won't be selling the flat Mike," I said.

"But I told them that I would be selling the flat and it would pay off all the debts." he was pleading now and I thought he looked pathetic.

"I spoke to your father this morning," I said and Mike sat at the kitchen table with his head in his hands. "Your father told me that this is not the first time you have been in trouble with gambling. What you may not know, Mike, is that this flat is in my name, not yours. Your father knew what might happen. He told me that if you ring him he will pay your debts but that would be the last time."

I reached across the table and held his hand. "You need help Mike," I said. I also looked up Gamblers Anonymous, and found their number for you." I slid the paper across the table.

"You bitch!" he said surprisingly. Then he stood up. "I bet you were fucking my father, that is why he put the flat in your name. I don't have a problem, you do. Whore!"

Mike slammed the door on his way out of the flat. Mike went to Glasgow and his father paid his debts again, so that was the end of it, I thought.

Spanked again by Miss Smith

Coming to the conclusion that I was actually a lesbian made a huge difference in my life. It gave me permission to do all sorts of things that I wanted to do, but thought I shouldn't. On the bus to work the next day I started to look at other girls without feeling guilty. That's okay now, it is in my nature to look at girls. During my lunch break, I looked at lesbian websites without feeling guilty, and in the evening I looked at all sorts of videos on the internet seeing what sort of lesbian I am. It was fun and I must say I was a little sore in the morning with all that activity. It turns out I am a submissive lesbian who likes anal games and who likes to be spanked. I am happy with that.

It is hard to believe what a relief it was for me to know myself, and be relaxed about it.

With Mike out of the flat, I had plenty of time to study and I studied hard. By the time I went to see Miss Smith again I was really on top of the work she had planned for me. I got a message from her to say that we should meet at her house and not at her office. She had given me her address and it was only a short walk, so I arrived at seven in the evening as I was told to do.

Miss Smith met me at the door and invited me in. The house was a lovely small detached house, in an old area. It had a very warm feeling about it with small rooms and quaint little alcoves that Miss Smith or her partner had filled with all sorts of nick-nacks. "Oh how lovely," I said as Miss Smith invited me into the small dining room. It took us an hour to go through the work she had set for me and at the end she said. "Well Done Madison, You're really getting the hang of all this."

Miss Smith was packing up the books when I said. "So no spanking this evening then?" but I was obviously disappointed.

"No," Miss Smith said. "You have done very well, you are a good girl, so no need for another spanking."

We were walking towards the door when I had an idea. "Miss Smith?" I asked.

"Yes, my dear,"

"Is there such a thing as a good girl spanking?" I said.

Miss Smith turned me around in the narrow corridor at the front door. Looking me straight in the eyes she asked. "Did you like it when I spanked you last time?" I just nodded, looking down at my feet.

"Well," she said after some thought. "I have to go out now and meet my partner for dinner, but I am alone over the weekend, she is going to see her mum. Why don't you come over on Saturday afternoon and we will find out what a good girl spanking is all about."

I was thrilled as I walked back to my flat, and it never occurred to me that Miss Smith's partner might not appreciate her spanking my bottom.

I was so excited on Saturday I didn't know what to do first. I was up early and bathed. I then decided that I should shave to make me look younger maybe. I had no idea what other lesbians liked. I know this sounds silly but it was what I was thinking at the time. I just wore a little makeup, I didn't want to look tarty. My long blond hair always took time and I considered pigtails but that was going too far I thought, so I brushed it out straight. I wore white knickers to go under my favourite short white dress and no bra. I didn't want the extra straps on my shoulders. I looked in the mirror, I was ready. But it was only ten in the morning. I plonked myself down in the lounge and picked up a book to read. Then I made some tea. Then I switched on the TV and watched Golf. That reminded me of Mr Hunter and the way he has looked after me. Such a nice man, except when he spanked me that time when we were on our own. Since then he has certainly made up for it. I looked at the clock, ten-thirty.

I just hung around until midday. One minute passed,

It was afternoon so I walked to Miss Smith's lovely little house and knocked at the door. Miss Smith was wearing a tracksuit when she opened the door. "Look at you," she said, running her eyes from my feet to the top of my head. "Don't you look good enough to eat?"

I giggled in anticipation.

I had decided to wear my flat shoes instead of heels, so as I walked in Miss Smith towered over my five foot two inches. Miss Smith was talking again. "I know I said in the afternoon, but I am ot sure I was expecting you to come this early. Never mind, let's go into the lounge and have some tea."

I hadn't been in the lounge when I came here last time, and it was lovely. I sat on the settee and Miss Smith offered me tea, which I declined. She was so nice. We talked for hours about things. She was interested to hear about my life and all the things that had happened recently, and I was interested in her as well. At about two she asked the question that she had wanted to ask. "So, you are no longer with your husband. Do you have a boyfriend?"

"No," I said. "I think I am off boys forever."

"Girlfriend then?" She asked.

"No, not that either, but I am hoping to find one soon," I said. I took a deep breath. "After Mike left for Glasgow I had a good long look in the mirror. I had always thought I was normal, you know, heterosexual. But recently I have changed my mind. I am pretty sure I am a lesbian."

"Are you?" Miss Smith said. "I do hope that nothing I have said or done has made you think that way."

"Well, no not really," I said. "But once I decided that, I knew it was right. I have been so happy over the last few days knowing that I love women and that is okay."

"Good Girl," Miss Smith said. "So I guess it is time for your good girl spanking."

"Oh yes please," I clapped my hands and then thought better of it.

Miss Smith laughed, then took my hand as she stood up. "Come on," she said.

We climbed the stairs and went into a small room at the back, which was probably the third bedroom or nursery. It was small and warm and had lots of things hanging on the wall. With a closer look, I discovered these things were whips and canes and all sorts of different implements designed to cause pain to the average naughty girl. There was a small massage table up against one wall and what looked like a tall trestle with a padded top and velcro straps around each leg. Cruising the internet recently I had looked with horror at people's dungeons but this room was not like that. This room had been built with love, I thought.

"What do you think?" Miss Smith broke the silence.

"I am not sure what to think. I am a little frightened and a little excited." I said. "Don't worry Madison, I am not a sadist, I am spanked in here more often than I do the spanking. My partner likes to spank my bottom, and other things of course. But you are new to all this so I thought I would show you what happens here." Miss Smith pulled out an ordinary dining chair from behind the door. "I think you are familiar with the use of one of these?" she asked.

"Well, they are for sitting on for dinner," I said smiling.

"That has earned you one extra stroke with the cane that you will receive later." Miss Smith was also smiling, but it was a different type of smile.

"Oh!" I said but decided to leave it there.

"This, my dear girl, was a very cleverly designed device for spanking naughty girls. I think it was later that someone else decided that there was a different use for it. If you put six of these around a table then we could eat together." Miss Smith sat down. "We always start with an ordinary hand spanking to warm the bottom. You would not like me to use any of the things hanging in the wall on a cold bottom."

"No," I said carefully. "I can see that."

Miss Smith sat down. "Come on my girl, I think I

would like to spank your bottom for you."

"Right," I said.

"Oh no, you say, "Yes Miss." when I give you a command, and you do it straight away, just like my girls did when I was a teacher."

"Yes, Miss," I said as I bent over her lap.

"Good Girl."

Then Miss Smith smoothed my short dress down over my small bottom. "I was just thinking last time I spanked you, what a lovely bottom you have. It is a pleasure to spank."

I was pleased with the compliment and said, "Thank you, Miss."

Lifting up my dress she said. "Time to unwrap my present I think." then she gasped. "Oh, white cotton knickers, my favourite, how did you know? I was going to bare your bottom for the first spanking but now I am going to leave these on. I love white knickers."

With that, Miss Smith started spanking. She was spanking my bottom quite hard straight away, harder than I expected for a warm-up spanking. Her small hand came down over and over again and I am sure I would be crying before she finished if she carried on like that. Very soon, however, she stopped and lifted up the side of my knickers to see the result. "Very nice," she said. "Let's have these down now, shall we," she said as she lifted the elastic at the top of my knickers. "Lift up for me, little angel,"

I lifted my bottom off her lap so that she could lower my knickers and then she took them right off. "Good girl," she said as she stuffed the knickers into the pocket of her tracksuit. "Now the spanking starts."

"Oh, God!" I thought to myself. "Has the spanking not started?"

Miss Smith's hand was small and when she spanked my small bottom she only spanked on one cheek or the other, or the tops of one leg or the other. She would spread the spanks all around my poor bottom and I never knew what was coming next. On the whole, however, I think she did a good job when I looked in the mirror a little later, the red stain was spread evenly over my whole bottom and the tops of my legs. And it really did sting.

"Up you get now," Miss Smith said when she stopped. "Time for a break." Miss Smith stood up, "Not for you of course, for me. You don't get a break, after all, I am doing all the work. Slip off your dress and then go and stand facing that wall over there. Put your hands on your head and your nose against the wall." She came up behind me and slipped a piece of paper under my nose. "Hold that there with your nose Madison, if I find it on the floor it will be extra with the cane later."

"Yes Miss," I said, but the moment I said that the paper slipped down.

"Not easy is it?" Miss Smith said but I had the good sense to keep quiet.

Miss Smith was wearing trainers and the floor was carpeted so I was not sure if she was in the room or not. I didn't dare look to find out. It may have been ten minutes with my nose against the wall or thirty, I had no way of knowing.

Suddenly there was a voice behind me and Miss Smith took away the piece of paper. "Such a good girl. I always lose the paper two or three times when I have to stand where you are standing."

I was rather proud of managing to do that when Mis Smith couldn't. "Thank you," I said.

"Now little angel," Miss Smith said. "We will try the trestle. It is quite high so you will probably have to be on your tiptoes. Over you go and get comfortable, not that you will be comfortable for long," Miss Smith laughed.

I stretched up and over the trestle. I was worried that it might not take my weight but it was very strong and sturdy, so my weight and even someone with twice my weight, would not be a problem. Miss Smith was right about the height, however, When I stretched over the soft cushion at the top, I could just reach the floor with my hands but my tiptoes

PAULA MANN

were off the floor at the back. When I leaned back a bit so that my tiptoes were just touching the floor, I lost balance with my hands.

"Don't worry little angel," Miss Smith said. "I am going to attach your hands and your feet to the sides of the trestle so both will be off the floor, then you will be stretched over with your little bottom spread and on display."

I said nothing, but I wondered what I had got myself into. I was just expecting a spanking, not a visit to the dungeon. Miss Smith was busying herself by attaching the velcro around my wrists and I lost balance again. She held me in place and went around the back to attach my ankles. I was now totally bound and exposed. Miss Smith could do what she wanted.

Don't worry my angel, this is not as bad as it feels right now, and a little later it will be amazing. More spanking first, I think." I lifted my head up to see what Miss Smith was doing and she seemed to be making a decision. "Hum," she said looking around the items hanging on the wall, "So many choices," Then she took off the wall a piece of wide leather that was split into three tongues. "This is called a tawse, Madison. If you were born in Scotland you would know more about the tawse, would you like to know what it feels like?"

"Not really, Miss Smith," I said. I was really worried.

28

"That little remark has earned you an extra stroke of the cane, Madison." Miss Smith said. "I think if you can't say anything positive I suggest you don't say anything at all." I kept my mouth shut.

I couldn't see what was happening behind me but I felt the breeze just before I heard the sound of the crack of the tawse on my bottom, and then I felt the pain. I am sure there was only a millisecond between them but I remember three distinct sensations. I let out a scream. The tawse wasn't like the cane, the pain was spread out rather than concentrated in one burning line, and I don't think it was as painful as the cane, but it made me scream anyway.

"Try not to scream my angel," Miss Smith said. "This room is padded so very little sound gets out but still, we don't want to alarm the neighbours, do we?"

I shook my head no, but tears were already falling off my cheeks onto the carpet. The tawse landed again and I didn't make a noise. I knew what to expect now, and it wasn't all that bad, really. I think that Miss Smith was giving me the worst one first. Everything after that was not bad. "Well, that was the tawse, what do you think little angel?" I just nodded, I didn't trust myself.

Miss Smith was looking around the room again. "Oh yes," she picked up something from the wall. "This is called a flogger. Lots of little stings instead of one big one. It can be a lot of fun as well, depending on who uses it, I guess. Do you want to try it?"

I looked over my shoulder as best as I could and I caught her eyes. She was smiling and I just nodded. "There you go, little angel. That was easy wasn't it."

I didn't have to wait long to feel the flogger. It seemed to be in constant motion flicking its ends into all my nooks and crannies. It started on my back. I have never been punished on my back and I knew I wouldn't like it, but I did. I liked it a lot. The whippy parts of the flogger landed all over my back and as soon as I felt one piece catch me as it flicked around under my breast, I felt another on the other side of my body. The emotional response was intense. I was not crying from the pain. I was crying from the emotional release of the last few days.

"Are you alright little angel?" Miss Smith was concerned but I just nodded.

After another ten minutes with the flogger, Miss Smith loosened the ties around my ankles and wrists and told me to stand up. "Sit on that wooden bench over in the corner, I am going to get us both a coke." I sat down and then stood up straight away, Miss Smith must have seen me because I heard her laughing as she went to the kitchen. I sat back on the bench gingerly as Miss Smith walked back in carrying two glasses of fizzing coke. "There you go," she handed one to me and I discovered I was thirsty.

"Time for you to tell me all about it I think." Miss

Smith said. I just nodded and then told her the deeper stories. My submissive husband, the gambling, my father-in-law and when he spanked me. Everything. Miss Smith just sat beside me on the bench holding my hand. "So now you are a lesbian because you have had bad experiences with a couple of men," she said.

"No, you don't understand," I said. "I think I have always known I am a lesbian but I was brought up to think it was a deviation from what is normal. When you said you were a lesbian I realised that you were normal just like anybody else."

"Well," Miss Smith said, "I think that depends on your definition of normal, doesn't it."

I nodded, deep in my own thoughts.

"Okay little angel, I am now going to take you to the moon and back." Miss Smith was standing now and looking for something in the cupboard on the far wall. "Ah," she said, as she came out with some cuffs and cable. "Lie on the table over there, and trust me, you are going to love this. Well, you will hate it at first but then you will love it." She was laughing at her own joke, but that didn't make it any better.

I clambered up on the table and laid on my back as Miss Smith clipped cuffs around my ankles and wrists, then she picked up a plastic rod that she called a spreader and connected the ankle cuffs to it, spreading me very wide. Then the wrist cuffs were attached as well so I had my legs spread wide in the air feeling the breeze on my sensitive anus and pussy. Picking up the flogger again she used it all over the exposed parts of my body. It really stung, particularly on my pussy, but the sting was turning to excitement every time it landed. The flogger had a way of getting into everything. Creeping around corners and slipping between places that are normally hidden.

Miss Smith put the flogger down and used her hands to spank my pussy. Then she spanked my anus and I said, "Yes."

"Oh," she said. "My little angel likes her anus spanked does she?" I shook my head "no", but at the same time, I lifted my bottom to offer her a better target. "Ah," she said. "The head says no but the body says yes." She spanked me there again and again. I was crying with the pain and continued to lift my bottom higher.

Tears were rolling down my cheeks as Miss Smith picked up the flogger again. I was not sure I could take any more, but Miss Smith knew I could. She seemed to know me better than I knew myself. Finally, she put down the flogger and came to the top of the table and kissed me full on the lips. This was my first real lesbian kiss. It was amazing. Who knew that kissing should be like this. I will never kiss a man again, I thought to myself. And, as it happens, I never have.

As Miss Smith kissed me she reached down my body and cupped my stinging pussy. The pain of the sting instantly turned into pleasure. "You are soaking wet, little angel." Miss Smith said. "I think you enjoyed our little spanking games. I raised up my bottom again and she guessed what I wanted. Fingering my anus using the moisture from my pussy she pushed a finger inside of me, then two. At the same time, she sucked in my nipple and bit it. I couldn't hold back, I came instantly pumping my bottom up and down to push the fingers in deeper. It was an amazing orgasm, as good or better than the ones I experienced with my landlady last year. As soon as it reached its high point, I think I must have passed out.

When I came too I was just lying back on the table and the cuffs had been removed. I was a mess. I sat up carefully and said. "Thank you, Miss Smith. That was amazing, but you forgot the cane."

"I haven't forgotten little angel, you can have it next time," she said.

"Will there be a next time?" I said.

"I hope so, my little angel," she said and then she kissed me deeply.

It was six o'clock when I got back to my flat, and I had no idea where all that time had gone. I was still a little unsteady but I managed to get back alright.

Spanked by Mrs Trent

I continued to go to Miss Smith to report the progress with my studying, but I was doing so well now that I never needed a punishment spanking and I was beginning to miss it. While she would go through the work that I did she made me stand next to her, and she would run her hand up and down my leg, going right to the top sometimes. I stopped wearing knickers for these occasions and the first time she noticed it she said, "Naughty Girl", and continued reading my work as she played with my bare pussy.

That's as far as it went with my lessons. It was very frustrating and I had to go home and finish myself off every time. On one occasion when I was just about to leave, I said. "Miss Smith, please can I have another good girl spanking from you?"

"Of course, my little angel," she said. "Come over on Saturday afternoon like before and I will help you then."

"Thank you, Miss Smith," I said, and I found myself skipping on the way home.

I spent as much time preparing myself as I did last time and was at Miss Smith's door at about ten past twelve. Imagine my surprise when Mrs Trent answered the door. "Yes," she said and obviously didn't recognise me.

"Oh, Hello Mrs Trent," I said. "I was expecting to see Miss Smith, she said that I should come here this afternoon."

"Well you had better come in then, go and sit in the lounge, do you know where that is?" she said.

I was tempted to tell her that I would prefer to wait in the small bedroom upstairs, but I held myself back. I sat on the settee and brushed my white dress down. "How long will she be, do you think?" I asked Mrs Trent.

"I have no idea," Mrs Trent said. "But if she said that she would be here, I expect she won't be long."

"Has she gone out with her partner?" I asked.

"Her partner?" Mrs Trent was obviously angry. "I am her partner. What do you think I am doing in this house? I own the house and Miss Smith lives with me."

"Oh, I am sorry," I said. "I didn't know."

"No," Mrs Trent said. "I don't expect you did. So what has Sarah Smith been telling you? I bet she told you that she was the head of this household and her partner does as she is told. Well, do I look as if I am someone who would do as I am told?"

"Um, no Mrs Trent," I said. But the conversation was getting very awkward so I started to get up.

"Where do you think you are going?" Mrs Trent said in a voice that you didn't argue with. "You just sit back down again, I want a few words with you. I expect you were coming here to get a spanking from Miss Smith weren't you? I will have a few words with Sarah when she gets back and those words will be with her bent over and me using a cane on her bottom. I know what she gets up to when I am not here. She is such a naughty girl. So, did she spank you?"

I thought I had better lie. I didn't want Miss Smith to get into trouble. "No, of course not." I lied. "She is helping me with my studies."

"I don't believe you, what's your name?" Mrs Trent said.

"Madison Hunter," I said.

"Madison Hunter?" Mrs Trent was thinking. "Oh yes. You were that little girl who cried in my office and I sent you to Sarah to get some education." She said but was continuing to think. "I remember now. You failed that exam, Sarah told me, and I said that the next time I see you I will put you over my knee and spank your naughty bottom. Wasting all our time and not studying hard enough."

I knew I was guilty of that, so I said. "Yes, I am sorry, Mrs Trent. But I am doing better now."

"I bet that is because Sarah spanks you. Does she spank you?" Mrs Trent asked again. "And make you stand next to her so that she can run her hands up your skirt while she reads your work like she did when we were teachers together. Does she do that?"

"No Mrs Trent. She never did that." I lied again.

"I don't believe you," she said. "Anyway, I had better give you that spanking I promised you for failing that exam. Get that skirt up and get over my knee."

I knew I was cornered, and I just hoped Miss Smith would arrive home soon and save me, although I am not sure what she could do. "Come on girl." Mrs Trent said. "I am going to give you that spanking you should have had from your teachers at school. I have had a lot of experience dealing with naughty girls like you."

I stood up and walked towards her, raising my dress right up. Mrs Trent patted her lap and it was then I noticed that she had sat on one of the dining chairs. She must have expected to be spanking me this afternoon. I bent over her lap and she started to spank me straight away, hard and fast. Then she took the elastic of my knickers and eased them over

37

my bottom. "Lift up," she said.

My knickers were down around my ankles as she started to spank my bottom again. Mrs Trent was a good spanker, making sure every part of my bottom was covered. I was getting sore but I could feel I was also getting horny. When the spanking was coming to an end Mrs Trent started to massage my bottom very gently. It was lovely so I eased my legs apart hoping to encourage her to massage me there. "Not yet, my little angel." Mrs Trent said. Let's wait until Sarah comes home. I knew then that I had been set up. How else would she know Miss Smith calls me "little angel". While I was thinking about this the front door slammed and Miss Smith came into the lounge to find me bare bottom over Mrs Trent's lap.

"Hello Mary," she said as she leant over me to kiss her partner. "And hello little angel, I see you are getting your bottom spanked again."

"I have just started spanking her for failing that exam," Mrs Trent said. "But she still has to get the cane for lying, you know how I feel about lying."

"Lying?" Miss Smith said. "Oh yes, we can't have any lies. What was she lying about?"

"She told me that you had never spanked her." Mrs Trent said. "And we never got onto that orgasm you gave her, and I expect she would have lied about that as well."

I had finally had enough and I said, "Hey, that's not

fair." It is hard to be indignant when you are bare bottom over someone's knee, but I did my best.

"I know it's not, little angel," Mrs Trent said with her hand on my bottom. "We are just having some fun at your expense. I hope you don't mind."

"And, by the way." Miss Smith joined in. " I am very proud of you for trying to defend my honour. Mary said that you probably wouldn't lie to save me, but I said you probably would. And the bet was a "get out of spanking free card". So thank you for that." Then she leaned forward and kissed me full on the lips.

Mrs Trent patted me on my bottom and said. "Well that was the starter, I think it is time we got on with the main course, don't you? Stand up Madison and let's go upstairs. And you can strip as well Sarah, you are going to get such a spanking."

"Yes Miss," she said.

Miss Smith and I were sent to the small bedroom upstairs where I had been spanked over the trestle. The room was just the same and as we were both naked, it seemed appropriate for us to hug, and then kiss, and then cup each other's pussies until Mrs Trent came in wearing just a bra and knickers. She was carrying a hairbrush which she used on our bottoms to get our attention.

It was an amazing afternoon that ran into the evening, and I think I felt all of the punishment implements hanging on the walls. Mrs Trent certainly knew how to spank a girl's bottom and she never tired of spanking both Miss Smith and I.

The finale was with Miss Smith and I, bent over the table side by side getting twelve strokes of the cane on our bare bottoms. Each stroke landed on all four cheeks but as Miss Smith was on my right-hand side, I think she got the worst of it.

Finally the three of us ended up in the king size bed in the master bedroom making love. I was guided by Mrs Trent to help Miss Smith achieve an orgasm, with my face on her pussy sucking her clit. At the same time Mrs Trent was behind me with her finger in my anus, and her other hand pinching my nipple. I came at the same time as Miss Smith, not the first for the day and I didn't expect it would be the last. Then we both attacked Mrs Trent, moving around her body bringing her to the brink, but not letting her cum. "Oh God," she said. "Do I have to take the cane to your bottoms again, I can't stand it, finish me off." So we did. I was exhausted and fell asleep quickly but they were happy to lay there holding each other.

The following morning Mrs Trent came in with a tray of tea at eight o'clock and spanked the bottom that was sticking out from under the covers.

"Ouch," Miss Smith said, waking up from her sleep. "I am sore."

"I know," Mrs Trent said. "If you both get on your

knees I will rub some cream onto your sore bottoms."

Miss Smith was the first in place and I was right beside her. Mrs Trent was very good with the cream and eventually was no longer easing the pain on our bottoms, but massaging our pussies. Mrs Trent knew what she was doing and while I had no idea how Miss Smith was getting on, I had Mrs Trent's four fingers playing with my little clit and her thumb buried deep inside me. I quickly had a wonderful orgasm.

After that incident with my teachers, I was a confirmed lesbian, out of the cupboard and in the open. I visited my teacher friends often. During the week I would be there next to Miss Smith while she checked my work with her hand up my skirt and on my naked bottom. Sometimes on the weekends I would join them in the small bedroom upstairs, and go home with a very sore bottom and a smile on my face.

I passed my basic and my advanced HR exams, and Mrs Trent suggested that I am now ready to get a better job. She had arranged an interview with the owner of a recruitment company, Mrs Bottoms (I am not making this up), and I got the job. Mrs Bottoms was a large lady in both stature and personality, with short silver grey hair and a large bottom and breasts. She welcomed me at the interview with a hug, which was a good start, and when I sat down across the desk from her, she mentioned that I had glowing references from Mrs Trent. The rest of the interview was a walk in the park, and I walked away from there with a job offer, which I accepted.

But that, as they say, is another story. If you would like to know more about what happens to Madison Hunter, read the next story in this series "The Strict Boss"

The End
Paula Mann
xxx

If you have enjoyed this book please don't forget to give it a star rating and leave a comment. Thank you

Visit our site to see all the spanking books: https://www.spankingbooks.com/ You can also subscribe to this site to get advanced notice of books coming out in the future and free spanking stories when we write them.

Please feel free to write to the authors with suggestions or ideas. If the authors like the ideas they may write the book you suggest and then send you a free copy for your enjoyment.

Peter Michaels - peter@spankingbooks.com
Pamela Michaels - pamela@spankingbooks.com
Paula Mann - paula@spankingbooks.com

Aunty Mae's Punishment Book Series by Paula Mann

Aunty Mae's Punishment Book One 1960 to 1967
Aunty Mae's Punishment Book Two 1967 to 1971
Aunty Mae's Finishing School for Girls 1971 to 1972

Hampstead Court Tails Series by Paula Mann
> The Estate Agent and the Secretary
> The Journalist and the CEO
> The Professor and the Cleaner
> The Security Guard and the Heiress

Spanking Bedtime stories - By Paula Mann and Peter Michaels
> Naughty Neighbours one - Pat and Christine
> Naughty Neighbours two - Jenjen and Patricia
> The Girl Next Door one - Olivia and Miss Parkinson
> Mother and Daughter Spanked - Claire Bell and her daughter Samantha
> The Price she has to Pay - Layla Turnbull and her daughter Chloe
> The Final Price - Both Daughters are Spanked Together
> The Travelling Salesman 1
> The Travelling Salesman 2
> The Strict Landlady
> The Strict Mother-in-law
> The Strict Teachers
> The Strict Boss
> The Strict Lover

Sting by Paula Mann

Peter & Pamela's Domestic Discipline Series

An American Houseguest by Peter Michaels
Anika's Education by Peter Michaels
The List by Peter and Pamela Michaels
Pamela Discovers Spanking by Pamela Michaels
Peter's Spanking Pastimes by Peter Michaels